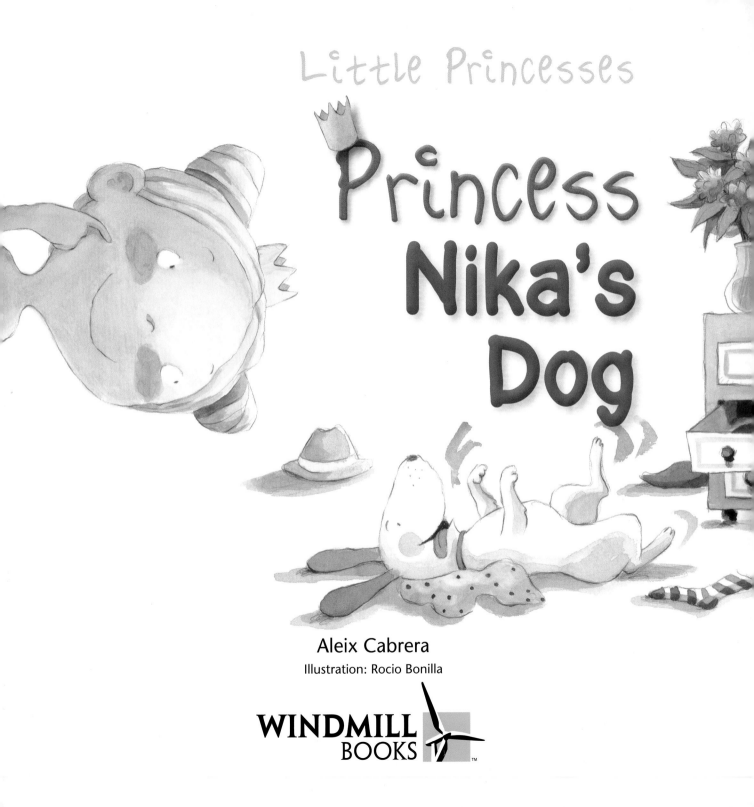

Little Princesses

Princess Nika's Dog

Aleix Cabrera

Illustration: Rocio Bonilla

WINDMILL
BOOKS
™

Aunt Margot enters

the Castle of Bricks with a little puppy in her arms and asks, "Can anyone take care of him?" "I want it! I want it!" repeats Princess Nika until her mouth is dry.

3

Princess Nika thinks that her new puppy, Cotton Candy,
will be the best accessory for her dresses, pearls, and sparkles.
She has no idea about pets, and if somebody told her that
dog poops come out decorated in wrapping paper,

she would believe it.

Nooooo!

6

But the princess soon

discovers that an animal is not a toy, that pets demand work and responsibility, and that puppies can cause more than one headache.

"Keep still!" she shouts at the dog. "Leave my hair alone! Do you know how many hours I spent at the hairdresser's?"

8

The puppy doesn't know what he can play with and what he can't. He rolls happily among the dresses and jackets.

"Oh no!" groans Nika. "You've covered my navy blue coat in hair! I'll look like **a sheep instead of a princess!**"

Oh no! When the dog discovers

the shoes, he bites them and smothers them with slobber as if they were candy. The princess's steps go "slip-slop," leaving a trail behind her. She even slips every now and then.

But what bothers the princess most is the puppy's smell. It's no use spraying the rooms and hallways with the best perfumes. Everything smells like the dog: the curtains, the quilt, the pillows, even her.

"They'll think **I'm a peasant!**

How embarrassing!"

Cough cough!

13

Fed up with the puppy,

Nika decides to take him very far away without telling anybody.

"I know a forest at the edge of the skyscrapers," she explains to him. "You'll be fine there, you'll see. I'm sure you'll make friends."

Disguised so that nobody can recognize her, the princess runs through the streets of the city until she leaves the sound of the people and cars behind her. "I don't imagine you'll be able to return to the castle from here, poor thing!"

she says **to the dog.**

"**Now** **you don't need** anybody
to take you for a walk, or anybody to pick up your
poops," she explains. "You're free! Go away!"
The little puppy remains still and sadly watches
Princess Nika, who moves away as the sun hides
behind the buildings.

Night falls and there aren't many streetlamps beyond the Castle of Bricks. Nika is not used to going out alone. Everything is so dark and all

the streets look the same. "I'm lost!"

It is night, an icy wind is blowing and on top of that, it starts to rain. The princess feels very sad and lonely. She starts to regret what she has done. "Poor Cotton Candy! Where will he be now? I want to go home…" she whines.

drip-drop

drip-drop

drip-drop

23

In the middle of the black night, the puppy runs towards Nika like a shooting star and barks twice. He is happy to see her and **wags his tail enthusiastically.**

The princess happily pets

Cotton Candy and thanks him for not being angry with her. At least they are together, although they are still lost far from home.

"What a mess I've got us in!" she mutters worriedly. "Will we get out of it?"

As if he understands her words, Cotton Candy goes down the street, turns left, then right, then around a corner and… In a blink of an eye, Princess Nika sees the Castle of Bricks in the distance! She jumps for joy.

"You've **found it!**"

"My friend, thank you for sticking by me," says the princess. "Do you know what? I don't care if I look like a hairy sheep, if my hair is frizzy, or if I slip all over the castle every now and then. I want you by my side always."

Published in 2018 by **Windmill Books**, an Imprint of Rosen Publishing
29 East 21st Street, New York, NY 10010

Copyright © 2018 Windmill Books

Text: Aleix Cabrera | Illustration: Rocio Bonilla | Design and layout: Estudi Guasch, S.L.

CATALOGING-IN-PUBLICATION DATA
Names: Cabrera, Aleix.
Title: Princess Nika's dog / Aleix Cabrera.
Description: New York : Windmill Books, 2018. | Series: Little princesses.
Identifiers: LCCN ISBN 9781508194590 (pbk.) | ISBN 9781508193999 (library bound) |
ISBN 9781508194637 (6 pack)
Subjects: LCSH: Dogs--Juvenile fiction. | Princesses--Juvenile fiction.
Classification: LCC PZ7.C334 Pri 2018 | DDC [E]--dc23

Manufactured in the United States of America
CPSIA Compliance Information: Batch BW18WM: For Further Information contact Rosen Publishing, New York, New York at 1-800-237-9932